"I was thoroughly pleased with the portrayal and use of Yamabuki's gender as well—the story avoids the usual traps of the 'female warrior trope' by keeping Yamabuki human, indeed sometimes gloriously androgynous, yet the fact she is a woman is essential to the story."

—*A. Hurst*

"[I]t makes medieval Japan come alive."

—*Nina Wouk*

"Katherine Lawrence writes with a very strong sense of place, of time, and of character. Yamabuki rides alone . . . depending on her own wit and ability to survive."

—*Anne Vonhof*

"[T]he last time I remember anticipating a next novel in this way was way back when, awaiting delivery of the next in Robert Van Gulik's Judge Dee series."

—*Aptos*

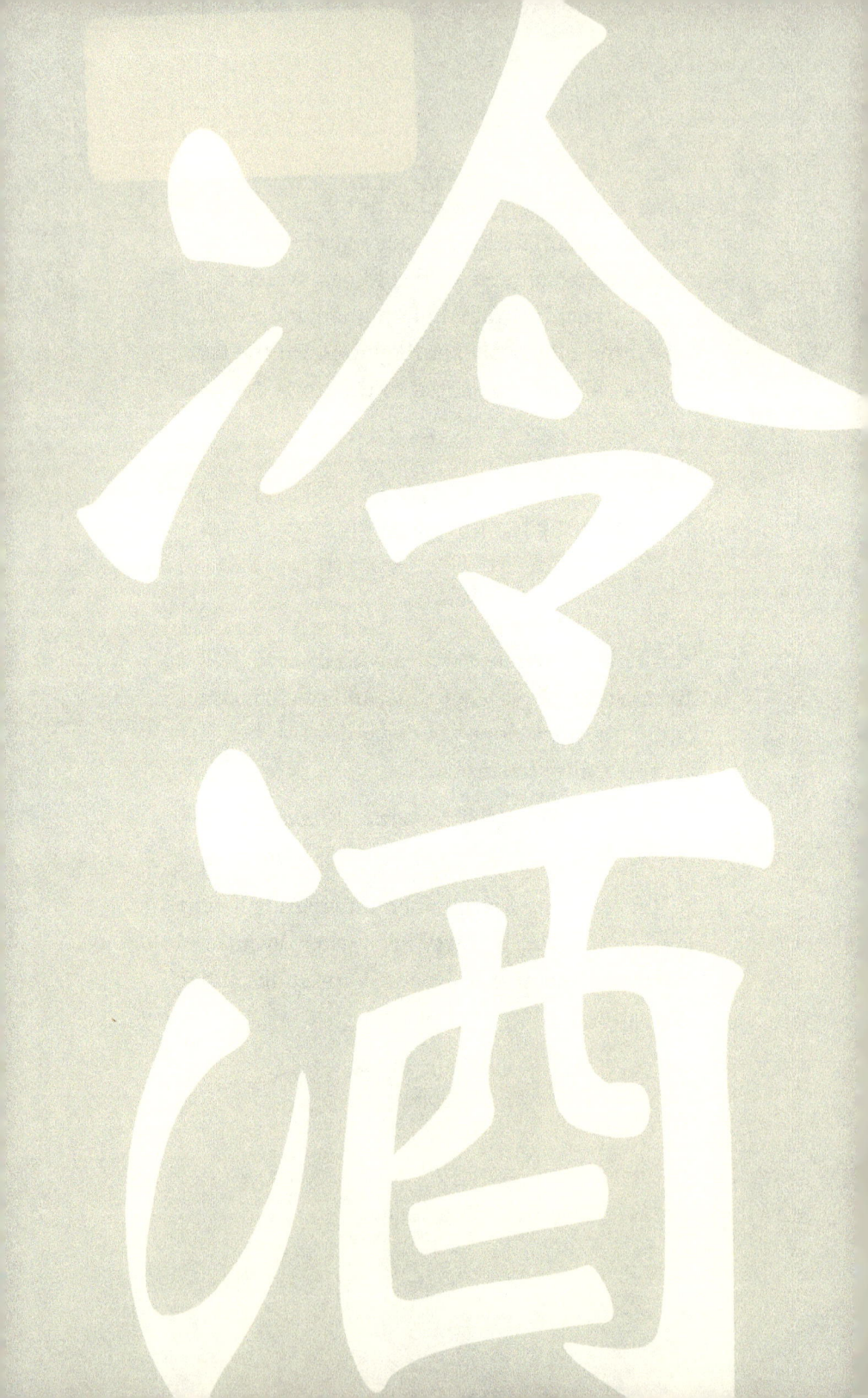

Cold Saké

Yamabuki vs. the Undead

A Novelette

Katherine M. Lawrence

Toot Sweet Ink
tootsweet.ink

Boulder

This is a work of fiction. All of the characters, organizations, and events portrayed in this novella are either products of the author's imagination or are used fictitiously.

A Toot Sweet Ink Book

Toot Sweet Ink is a trademark and imprint of Toot Sweet Inc.

Published by Toot Sweet Inc.
6525 Gunpark Drive Suite 370
Boulder, CO 80301

tootsweet.ink

@TootSweetInk

facebook.com/tootsweetink

Sign up for our Inkvine newsletter to get updates and learn about new releases and discount opportunities on our upcoming titles at http://eepurl.com/K8XVn

Library of Congress Control Number: 2014958746

First Edition

ISBN: 978-0-9912667-5-3 (hardback)

ISBN: 978-0-9912667-4-6 (paperback)

ISBN: 978-0-9912667-8-4 (ePub)

To Mildred Hale,
my fifth-grade teacher,
for her encouragement all those years ago.

ACKNOWLEDGMENTS

I would like to thank Martha F. Leaman, Nina Wouk, Taisuke Akasaka, Dana Densmore, Anne C. Vonhof, and my editor, Laura Scott, for their helpful suggestions and review of my draft manuscripts.

Contents

Long before it was called Japan,
the island empire was known
to the world as Akitsushima,
the Autumn Creek Land,
and among its samurai,
one of its mightiest warriors was
a woman named Yamabuki.

Cold Saké

THE PILLOW BOOK STORY

It is said that, more than a millennium ago, the Emperor of Hō sent a gift of two blank-paged books to the Emperor of Wa.

The Emperor of Wa kept one book for himself, whereupon he immediately began to write a story in the style of the scholars of Hō, for learned men of Wa greatly admired Hō and wished to emulate Hō in all things.

*The Emperor of Wa gave the
remaining book to his Empress.*

*"What shall I do with this?"
the Empress of Wa asked.*

*Her young attendant smiled.
"Use it as a pillow."*

ONE

THE OMENS ARE AGAINST YOU

Last day before Gods Absent Month
Five days after Dark Moon's Night
2nd Year of Shōan
October 31, 1172

THE DUSK PROMISED RAIN. The rider knew it, the horse sensed it, the sky foretold it. Behind her, what remained of the day clung to an unsettled horizon of dirty orange, jade green, and deepening blue. Ahead of her, the rutted road snaked northeastward—an unlucky direction.

The farmers back at Ogami village had assured her that she would reach East Wind Inn before sunset. Now it was past the Hour of the Monkey. She had ridden for over two hours without seeing so much as a hut.

Farmers! They'll say anything.

Near a washed-out bridge, the road detoured into a ravine where dead dry leaves danced about in small whirlwinds that carried with them the scent of autumn. She pulled her *jimbaori* cloak tighter, but still she shivered.

But then, as the road rose from the ravine, she spied a dark building in a shadowy grove of pines. A man stood near its entrance.

"We may have arrived at last, Mochizuki," she whispered to her mount. Yet as she rode further, she saw that it was not an inn at all, but an abandoned Buddhist temple. Probably built to guard the northeast direction from an approach by demons, it had fallen into ruin, overgrown by vines; its gardens lay choked in dead grass; its ponds sat putrid and muddy.

What she had taken for a man at the entry turned out to be a statue of Jizō—patron and guardian of dead children's souls. Entangled among vines, one of his arms was lifted, reaching for what scant light fell into the wooded grove. Carved in gray stone, Jizō's compassionate eyes stared into the gloom, his chiseled, serene expression sending a smile to the lone traveler. His other hand remained outstretched in an attitude of blessing, his shattered fingers bearing mute witness to the statue's decay.

The rider eased out of her stirrup and swung down from the saddle. In the undergrowth, near a twisted pine tree, she found a round, black rock about the size of her fist, which she placed before Jizō. *A rock to help the dead children escape the Yellow Land.*

Mochizuki neighed nervously. "Why are you nickering?" But before she finished speaking, she saw two riders approaching through the twilight. Weapons sheathed, they rode toward her at a canter.

In a single motion she swung back into the saddle.

The strangers slowed to a trot. If they were brigands, their armor likely would be a hodgepodge of looted pieces; yet, both of these riders wore elegantly matched sets of armor.

Probably samurai.

But that didn't mean they weren't a threat.

She sat straight up in the saddle, paying attention to every subtlety.

The strangers brought their mounts to a halt. "I am Shinjo Taro!" the elder warrior declared, raising his voice above the thump of hooves, pulling the woven blue silk cords of the bridle.

The comely one, the one who rode a half stride behind Taro, called out, "I am Sato Jiro!"

It was protocol for samurai to announce their names before a duel.

Do they seek combat?

"May we ask your name?" Taro's request was as much a command as it was anything.

"I am Taka Yamabuki!" she growled in answer as she had been taught, suppressing her female voice-range.

She eyed Taro—the dark and scarred one. His wild mane of hair could not conceal a grisly scar across his forehead. His forearms and face were likewise marked. Part of an ear was missing; two sword hand fingers, gone.

Fingers lost in battle, or forfeited for missteps?

Jiro looked at least ten years younger than Taro. For all of Taro's battle scars, Jiro was flawless and untouched.

Pretty.

He resembled a youthful courtier, or a young page; yet when their gazes met, she saw something icy and deadly lurking behind his eyes.

For a fleeting moment, she wondered if the two men were lovers. She knew that some warriors became emotionally drawn to one another. There was something about battle that forged these sorts of ties—deep ties. She pushed the thought aside. What they were to one another did not matter. She had to remain watchful. They were men; they were dangerous; and there were two of them.

Since they said nothing more, Yamabuki took it upon herself to continue in conversation. "Is there an inn on the road from which you came?"

Taro grunted. She took this for an affirmation.

"East Wind Inn?" she probed in the direct manner of a warrior.

Taro nodded, yes.

"So it's possible for me to be there before nightfall?" Though it was a question, her words were meant to show her determination.

Jiro spoke, his voice dark and beautiful. "Better to stay here, young warrior."

"No one stays at East Wind Inn anymore," Taro added with a sneer. "A haunted inn. Not even the priests can cleanse it."

Jiro smiled without mirth. "An inn named after an inclement wind, located on a road in an unlucky direction—the omens are against you." He looked askance at her, then raised his face up as if taking in a distant scent. "There is an approaching storm. If you get caught in the darkness, it could be your undoing."

She shook her head. "It is still the Hour of the Bird. There is still twilight."

"The forest is already dark. You might do better to stay at the Temple. They're havens for travelers. This one gives you shelter." Taro pointed at the dilapidated structure.

"Sleep in abandoned ruins?" She stiffened. "That's not what I had in mind. I don't believe in lucky or unlucky directions, nor, for that matter, in ghosts or demons—stories priests tell to frighten children into obedience. Surely you don't think that warriors such as we would ever believe—"

"Oh!" Taro growled in challenge, his eyes growing small and fierce.

Yamabuki held her tongue. This was not worth shedding their blood. She answered in a measured voice, "I am tired. I have ridden all day and I would spend the night with Emma, the Regent of Hell, himself, if he had strong saké, good rice, and a warm bed."

"You may well get your wish, young samurai," Taro warned in a low voice. "You have been warned. As the saying goes, 'A road northeast leads to an encounter with the Ushi-Tora.'" He threw back his head, giving out a sinister laugh.

They seem overly eager to have me stay.

"And a saying also goes," she replied, " 'If even a wise emperor makes mistakes, then what can be expected of ordinary subjects?'" With that she wheeled Mochizuki about and headed northeast.

"Good luck, Taka Yamabuki!" Jiro cried.

She looked over her shoulder, but they were nowhere in sight.

She rode on, alone.

Two
YOU NEED MORE SAKÉ, WARRIOR

I T WAS AT the Hour of the Dog, when the night had fully fall-
en, before East Wind Inn at last came into view. Its peaked
thatched roof loomed above the trees along a long lonely stretch
of road. Larger than she expected, although smaller than the es-
tate house in which she was raised, the inn looked like it had
started out as a farmhouse, but had grown over time.

As she approached, a pallor of gloom pervaded everything.
Continually out of the corners of her eyes, Yamabuki detected
a darting movement; yet upon looking more closely, everything
remained still. Though stone lanterns burned brightly, they
seemed unable to penetrate the dark. Though the paths seemed
well tended, they did not look clean. Though the structures were
looked-after properly, they were not welcoming.

Everything was totally right, while at the same time totally
wrong.

Where is everyone? Why have I not been greeted?

And as if someone had overheard her, a man with a crackled
voice cheerfully called out from afar, "Welcome, samurai-sama, welcome." Seemingly from nowhere, a wiry, gray-haired

man scurried toward her. The elder man bowed low. "I'm called Mikiyasu."

Finely dressed, he put on an air of congeniality, yet his eyes shone with angst.

"Please find our humble accommodations acceptable, samurai-sama." Mikiyasu was trying to ape the speech of the high-born, and even appended *sama* when he addressed her, a title reserved to those of lordly rank.

Am I so frightening?

A young boy, also nicely dressed, followed behind him, his smile genuine; an innocent smile.

"Hidashi! Take the young man's mount."

The boy bowed and stepped up to grasp Mochizuki's halter.

"Innkeeper," Yamabuki said dismounting, "I am looking for strong saké, good rice, and a warm bed."

"Kinu," the old man cried to someone inside the inn, "prepare some food and saké for our guest! He will be staying with us tonight!"

Yamabuki was amused by the innkeeper's assumption. Being a warrior, she had deliberately chosen the direct speech pattern of men. And as a young woman traveling alone in the *oku*, it served her purposes that, in her armor, Yamabuki outwardly was not unlike any other warrior.

Collecting Mochizuki's reins, the boy smiled wryly.

"Do you have stables and food for my horse?" the warrior asked the boy.

He bowed with formal humility. "Stables and food, which we hope are worthy."

She turned her attention back to the innkeeper, who was

smiling so hospitably that she thought his mouth might break. "How much do you charge for meals and lodging for me and my colt?" Tired as she was, she had been advised it was best to ask innkeepers such questions before proceeding.

The smiling man immediately quoted her a ridiculously low figure. She paused for a moment to absorb this, and while she was thinking, he bowed low and dropped the fee further. Now she waited on purpose. Twice more he decreased the fee while increasing the services.

At last she said, "Innkeeper, better stop now or you'll end up paying *me* for your hospitality."

The old man blanched.

She continued, "But so long as the saké is strong, the rice is good, and the bed is warm, you will be paid fairly. Now stop your prattling before my ears go deaf."

Yamabuki removed her battle helmet and her glistening black hair fell down her back.

The innkeeper gasped. He quickly started making absurd apologies that she did not wish to hear. Her mind was on the youngster and the colt, who were already halfway to the stables. She headed across the courtyard after them, leaving the old man talking to himself.

"Careful," she warned as she caught up to the boy. "My horse is not friendly."

"I'm able to handle him," he stated confidently. "I'm used to warriors' horses."

To her surprise, the stallion accepted the boy's lead without objection.

"How old are you, Hidashi?"

"I was born in the second Year of Hōgen," he answered with some pride.

Second year of Hōgen? That makes him two years younger than me. He can't be that old!

"So you're 15 years of age?"

Hidashi blushed and looked away.

Ah! He hasn't learned the years.

Few commoners knew numbers, or how to add, or how to name the years based on the reign of the divine Emperors, but that did not matter and she let it go. Second year of Hōgen or first year of Oho—to them what did it matter?

"So old and yet you have not learned to be careful of a battle horse?" she chided softly. "Battle horses are raised to fight. He could easily hurt you."

"See how I have my elbow at his neck and how I hold his bridle. He can't step on me or get loose," Hidashi said with confidence. "I'm able to handle him."

"He does seem to mind you; yet he is a battle horse. They are strong willed. He could break loose if he decided to."

"When I saw him, I knew he didn't wish to hurt me."

Yamabuki raised an eyebrow. "And how could you tell that?"

"By his bearing. Horses reveal their feelings by how they hold their ears; I can see he's not afraid of me, so why should I fear him?"

Yamabuki tilted back her head and laughed. "So, the fearless need not be feared!"

Hidashi smiled, trying to hide that he blushed.

"So, you have cared for other battle horses?"

Hidashi straightened with concealed pride. "*Hai*, but never so fine as this one."

Yamabuki mirrored Hidashi's smile like a mother lion, for indeed she had raised Mochizuki from a foal. "You are a good judge of horses, then."

After a moment he asked, "May I know his name?"

"His name can be written, *Full Moon*."

Yamabuki cast her gaze around the inn. "Are there no guests other than me?"

Hidashi looked away. "No, they don't come so often anymore." He opened the gate to a surprisingly ample stable and led Mochizuki inside. The humidity gave the air an extra pungency—that odd mixture of the sweet and rancid so familiar to those who spend their lives with horses. "Mochizuki will like it here," he assured. "Warm with plenty to eat."

"Hidashi," she asked as she removed Mochizuki's bridle, "will you tell me why people stopped coming to the inn?"

There was silence. Finally he said softly, "The inn is good, only . . ." He trailed off.

Yamabuki grinned. "A boy who is unafraid of the fearless is tongue-tied when it comes to telling me what just about everyone already seems to have heard."

"You have heard the stories, then?"

She removed the saddle and set it aside, addressing Mochizuki. "Both of us have heard, eh, friend?"

"And you aren't scared?"

"I am not one who gives much credence to stories of fantastical beings," she answered.

"Grandfather's afraid," Hidashi said in a low tone. "He's afraid to have guests stay, for they become frightened, but if they don't come, how are we to make our living?"

"A bad predicament," she agreed, sitting down to remove her dark green lacquered armor. "What makes the guests afraid?"

"Frightful things moving in the night."

"What do the guests see?"

"Most see nothing, but sometimes they hear sounds. A few see things that frighten them." He stared off at things unseen, not moving.

"Hidashi, tell me and my fearless friend here, how did this all start?"

He took a deep breath. "It was at the time of Rice Planting in Water Month. Business had been good. . . ."

Yamabuki nodded, encouraging him to continue.

He drew closer to her, speaking even more softly, as if by telling the story, he might bring on a recurrence.

"We heard wicked laughter, like someone who had lost her senses."

Yamabuki's eyes narrowed. "A woman, then?"

"Hai," Hidashi whispered. "But after that, the terrible wailing started."

Yamabuki paused to consider. "Some animals can make strange, mournful, almost human sounds. Rabbits can sound like babies."

Hidashi lifted his hand to indicate that there was more. "Finally, one night, some of the guests saw *it*." He said *it* in a deliberate and measured way, and fell silent, hesitating to say any more.

She gently helped him continue. "And these guests, they ran away?"

Hidashi nodded in affirmation.

"Others have seen *it* as well?" she asked in a whisper, as if sharing a secret.

Hidashi nodded, eyes round, the lantern flames flickering in his wide pupils.

Yamabuki's voice grew even softer. "And you have seen *it?*"

Once again he nodded.

"What did you see?"

"A floating light, the size of a torch, the brightness of the full moon."

"That hardly sounds frightening," she said flatly, stacking her armor next to her. "Unusual, perhaps, but definitely not frightening."

"That's what my sister says, but that's not what the samurai see."

Yamabuki rose, taking a brush to Mochizuki's jet-black mane. "The samurai see something else, then? Tell me, what do they think they see."

"A fiend." He paused searching for words. "An *oni* from the depths of the *jigoku* itself."

"A devil from hell," she restated matter-of-factly, with a note of skepticism.

But he grew emphatic. "The samurai say it's not human. It has fangs and a snout, and they say it's bright blue!"

"A man wearing battle armor is frightening. Sometimes battle armor is made to look almost other-worldly in order to strike terror into an opponent." She looked at Hidashi. "But you have chosen not to run away. Why?"

Hidashi grew bold. "I can't leave my sister. Kinu is brave and she says she'll stay. If my sister stayed and I ran away, people would laugh at me."

Yamabuki stopped brushing the stallion, then spoke softly to Mochizuki. "Well, it looks like you and I get to find out what all this fuss is about. You will be all right here alone, I suppose?"

Mochizuki gave a soft grunt and ducked his head to munch on some rice straw.

Yamabuki put down the brush and picked up her satchel.

"Hidashi, I am tired. Mochizuki needs to rest as much as I do and I pity the devil that chooses to disturb him."

Satisfied that her armor, bow, arrows, and *naginata*—a noblewoman's lance-like weapon used against attackers on horse back—were securely stored in the tiny armory, she headed across the lantern-lit outer courtyard as the first few drops of rain started to fall from pitch-black skies. She was armed, as usual, with her long and short swords, and was dressed in her comfortable *hakama*, which she had managed to keep clean and pressed despite the travails of her journey. The baggy split trouser-skirt was festive, with a dark green tortoise-shell pattern. Her straw-colored kimono carried her family seal: two hawk feathers inscribed in a circle.

In the very short time it took to cross to the inn, the rain had started to fall in earnest.

The innkeeper bobbed up and down. "Come. Come inside." He urged her toward the door. "Kinu! Come tend to our guest. Bring an umbrella!"

When the door slid aside, a girl carrying a lantern and rain parasol scurried to Yamabuki. Dressed in an elegant dark brown kimono with orange lining, she smiled at the warrior without meeting her gaze. Holding the umbrella as high as she could, she led the warrior to the *engawa* of the inn, where she removed Yamabuki's boots.

"Do you have a name, Inn Girl?"

"I am Kinu."

Yamabuki nodded slightly.

The girl bowed and slid an inner door aside and bade the warrior to enter.

Yamabuki took in the anteroom, which was large and resplendent, at least for a backcountry inn. All the other heavy outer
sliding doors were closed against the weather. The braziers and
hearth burned brightly, providing heat and a warm glow to the
room where many tables sat empty in what surely had been a busy
eating and drinking area in earlier times. Yamabuki sat at a table
closest to the fire.

Where is that saké that the innkeeper promised?

And as if her mind were being read, an inner door opened and
an older woman appeared with a tray and a small saké bottle. With
some ceremony, she poured the wine into a ornate drinking-bowl.

"Cold saké. Strong." The older woman did not bow, but nodded,
almost imperiously, yet without ever quite becoming haughty.

Yamabuki, without ceremony, quaffed the contents down in a
gulp. The older woman poured another round, which took the last
of the small bottle. "You need more saké, warrior. I will fetch it."
With that she moved toward the inner doorway.

Yamabuki asked, "Excuse me, may I learn your name?"

The woman turned, and answered softly and with a great deal of
dignity, "I am Haruyo."

Yamabuki put down her empty cup. "Kinu and Hidashi are your
children?"

"Hai," she answered and turned to walk away, saying, "You need
more saké, warrior."

Yamabuki chose the time to reflect. She found it easy to reflect
when drinking saké, and on an empty stomach, the cold saké went
straight to her head.

She wondered what was at the bottom of all these strange happenings that the two samurai back on the road and Hidachi just now had described. And if it was as terrible as was said, why did the innkeeper and the staff not leave, if not from the haunting by imaginary beasts, then from lack of business? Why did they stay on? It did not at all make sense.

This cold saké is exceptionally strong.

The rain began to fall even harder, drumming the roof with its beguiling sound, filling the air with its freshness. Alone with Kinu, Yamabuki asked, "So just the four of you live here?"

"Grandfather, my mother, my brother, and me. Hidashi told me that you've heard the stories of demons. He says you are not afraid of oni. Perhaps a samurai does not fear them, but the common folk most certainly do. Everyone has run away."

"Your father, then?" she asked incredulously.

"He died three winters ago." She looked pained, and Yamabuki regretted having brought it up.

Yamabuki continued on another tack. "There are no others at the inn?"

"No, samurai-sama. You are the only guest tonight."

The heavy wood sliding door rumbled aside as Haruyo returned. Kinu fell silent.

With a much larger saké flask, Haruyo promptly replenished the warrior's cup. Next she brought in hot food: cooked rice mixed with vegetables and other grains. Haruyo smiled politely as she placed the food tray before the warrior. "I hope you will like this meager fare."

Looking at the steaming food, Yamabuki tried to mask the depth of her hunger. She had not eaten since yesterday.

Haruyo also offered some cold vegetables with fermented sauce, all of which the warrior finished hungrily.

"Cold saké and a hot meal." Yamabuki smiled and belched politely in the custom of Hō.

"This way, warrior," Haruyo smiled. "Your bed chamber is this way." She slid aside another screen, leading the warrior further into the inn.

THREE
IF I DIE, I DIE WITH MY SWORD

I T WAS IN the Hour of the Pig that Yamabuki, led by Kinu and
Haruyo, arrived at the ample inner room where soft and warm
bedding awaited her. They left Yamabuki, who now readied herself
for the third fulfillment—a warm bed.

The rain fell in torrents, running down the roofs, filling the gut-
ters, flooding downspouts, and spilling into pools in the garden—a
drenching rain, a lulling rain, a rain that turned the ground into
mud. But it was not a cold rain. It carried with it the scent of
spring.

Odd that an autumn rain should be so spring-like.

The bed was a simple affair: batting laid out on the floor, covered by a futon. She set her sword down within easy reach should
she need it. She removed her outer kimono and, clad in only her
shitagi, she slid beneath the covers. Lulled by the sound of the
downpour, the warm meal and cold saké, she slipped almost immediately into blissful sleep.

She dreamt, and in her dreams she walked along a gossamer path.
The path wrapped its way through a fine garden. The garden looked
well tended and opulent, resplendent with trees in full flower.

Yamabuki found herself to be in the most bewitching cloudless night. A lustrous moon illuminated everything in pale white light. As she walked, she heard someone weeping. She found herself following the sound of sorrow. A garden path led to a small pond.

A woman dressed in finery sat near a stone lantern. As Yamabuki approached, the crying stopped. Yamabuki could not see her face—the woman was turned away. However, by the elegance of the woman's robes, Yamabuki knew without question that the woman belonged to the High Court. Therefore Yamabuki addressed her with the most scrupulous politeness. "Lovely lady, why do you weep?"

Still turned away from Yamabuki, the aristocratic woman again broke into sobs. "I am alone. What is to become of me?"

"Who are you?"

The high born lady did not answer, and now drew closer, despite the fact she did not move.

The woman's voice grew so near that it seemed to leave the dream and enter Yamabuki's bed chamber.

Yamabuki, now fully awake, heard the same voice. It was very close—not a dream. "Oh my beautiful samurai," the high-born woman gasped wantonly, turning directly toward Yamabuki.

Through the semi-darkness, Yamabuki took in the woman's features. Indeed the woman displayed both aristocratic and natural beauty, which she easily could use to her advantage. She reflected every detail of courtly appearance. Her face was powdered white with *oshiroi*. Her long hair fell below her waist. Eyebrows were painted on her forehead. She had not blackened her teeth according to the custom known as *haguro* to mark committed fidelity. Yamabuki thus deduced that the woman did not have a husband.

Yamabuki sat up as the stranger walked toward her, enticing. "I want to feel your body next to mine. Let us make love, the last sweet love, before dawn."

That shattered the warrior's trance. She was back in her bed chamber, yet the highborn woman was there as well. Yamabuki did not find anything odd in this change of scene. She stood up, pulling her outer kimono around herself. "I have no desire for this."

The inn grew ever more lonely. In every direction, complete darkness, save for the small fire in the brazier.

The woman implored, "I left my family. I left everything for you. I carry your child."

"Lady, I can assure you that you do *not* carry my child."

"There has never been anyone else but you. You know that I have never shared love with anyone but you, Kojiro."

"I am not Kojiro," Yamabuki said very deliberately.

"Oh, what is to become of me now?" The woman stretched out her arms, inviting Yamabuki into an embrace.

Yamabuki stepped back.

"Why do you recoil, Kojiro? Let's kill ourselves as we agreed." And seemingly from nowhere the woman produced a *tantō*, which she raised high. Even in the dim light, the polished steel edge gave off a bright glint.

Yamabuki adjusted her stance. *She means to attack me?*

But the woman did not attack. Giving out with a horrible shriek, she plunged the dagger point into her own neck, making a single downward cut.

Blood gushed everywhere. All the while she made frightful, spasmic, gurgling sounds—drowning in her own blood.

She collapsed moments later, whereupon she grew very still, slumping soundlessly forward. The only sound came from Yamabuki's breathing.

The room became darker and utterly silent save for the soft hiss of the brazier coals.

Yamabuki knew the particular scent of blood. The horrific cut glistened in the glimmer of the faint light. When a blade rents the length of a neck, death comes quickly. Called *jigai*, self-disposal was taught to all highborn children—an action of last resort.

The scent of blood grew more intense, but then the smell started to change, and no longer was it a whiff of freshly spilt blood, but took on the decided odor of corpse rot. Yamabuki's gorge rose, yet she bent down to get a closer look at the dead woman.

It was then the brazier sputtered, only dimming coals.

The corpse made a gurgling sound. Yamabuki sensed the body writhing.

Is she still alive? She can't be.

In the nearly total darkness, Yamabuki reached to touch the body.

Without warning, something grabbed her wrist, twisting with such force that it brought her to her knees. She fought to get loose, but in moments she was tossed onto her back. Now in the grip of something physically stronger than she, with her free hand the warrior struggled to grasp her sword, but it was not within reach.

Suddenly she felt the bloody tantō pressed against her own throat.

"Kojiro?" the voice gurgled. "Are you not going to follow me in death, as we agreed?"

Yamabuki, through clenched teeth, hissed, "Let me go."

"Why do you revile me?" the woman moaned, and at once whatever held Yamabuki released her. Yamabuki rolled away, not sure exactly where she was within the chamber. Her heart racing, she tried to get her bearings, feeling around for her sword.

It was then that what seemed like moonlight slowly began to fill the room; and what she saw filled her with horror.

The woman was no longer a fair and tragic young lady, but a *hannya*.

It slowly rose on its haunches. Yamabuki was tall—taller than most—but the creature was at least two heads higher than she. Yet it was not just its height that made it so fearsome, but its bulk— the bulk of an ox.

It glared at her, its yellow eyes filling with manic mirth, then bared its fangs—jagged razor-like protruding teeth.

Its crooked claw-like sharp-pointed fingers held the blood-stained tantō.

Yamabuki stood frozen.

The creature dropped the tantō at Yamabuki's feet, where it landed with a thud.

"This is for *you*, Kojiro." It snorted through a snout not unlike a boar's. Its teeth flashed. "Cut your throat with it."

Since the hannya stood between the warrior and her sword, Yamabuki fleetingly thought to grab the tantō and fight back, but that would bring her much too close to the powerful creature. And to stand and fight without weapons would be as futile as fighting a tiger bare handed.

In one motion, Yamabuki threw open the chamber door, running as fast as she could down the dimly lit hall.

The beast raced after her, lunging, almost on top of her; its claws lashed out. "You must die!" it growled.

Yamabuki narrowly avoided the talons. Running further, she saw an outside door looming ahead. She flung it open. A stabbing pain shot across her back as the oni's claws sank into her shoulder.

Yamabuki screamed as she leapt from the wooden planking into the outer courtyard.

She quickly tested her shoulders. *I can move my arms. It's only a scratch. I'll heal, if I live long enough.*

The rain fell in a pelting drive and within a matter of seconds she was soaked.

Guided by the flickering torches around the inn, she ran toward the stable's armory, but the hannya immediately intercepted her near a small cherry tree.

Yamabuki dodged, nearly slipping on a pile of wet leaves. The hannya grabbed for her, its long claws barely missing the warrior's face. Yamabuki stumbled, recovered, managing to maneuver so that the tree was between her and the hannya.

Someone yelled, "Samurai-sama!" It was Hidashi.

"Run, Hidashi! Run!" she yelled above the sound of the pouring rain.

He scurried toward the stables.

Suddenly the dagger appeared at Yamabuki's feet.

The hannya looked into her eyes. "This is for you, Kojiro! Fulfill your obligation."

Yamabuki bent down, as if to do what she was asked, but instead lunged and raced toward the armory.

In the gloom she could see Hidashi pulling the armory door open.

Yamabuki was fast, but the demon was closing ground, its feet spattering ever louder.

Yamabuki looked deep within herself for a final burst of speed.

The sound of their steps was suddenly joined by the hooves of Mochizuki as he thundered from the stable, fire in his eyes. In five great strides he was alongside her. Yamabuki was almost within the hannya's reach when she managed to grab onto the horse's mane and pull herself onto her mount, bareback. Commanding him only through the grasp of her fingers, she turned Mochizuki and jabbed her heels into his flanks. He kicked—his hind legs sent the hannya flying across the courtyard, where the monster rolled through the mud, landing against the side of the building with a dull thud.

To her surprise the demon stirred, picked itself up, and started in her direction.

Not waiting to see any more, Yamabuki turned her mount toward the armory.

In moments she was at its door. Leaping from Mochizuki's back, she slapped him on the rump, at which he bolted away.

"My bow and the arrow-keeper!" she demanded as if Hidashi was her page.

He handed her the *ebira* of arrows and the long bow.

She immediately selected one of the most lethal arrows, a crescent fork *ryokai*.

"Shoot it, Samurai-sama. Shoot it," he cried with a mixture of urgency and panic.

She notched the arrow, pulled the bow string tight and, aiming for the demon's eye, muttered, "And this is for you."

She released the arrow.

With a thump it lodged itself in the oni's neck.

"Missed!" Yamabuki spat.

She drew another arrow. Her aim true, the arrow struck the demon square in the eye, its point buried in the hannya's brain.

It snarled, "Am I not dead enough for you, Kojiro?" The demon started across the courtyard.

"The naginata!" she shouted.

Hidashi handed the polearm her.

"I shall cut the thing into pieces, alive or dead," she snarled through gritted teeth.

Emerging into the downpour, Yamabuki faced the approaching demon, and moved in at an angle. Her first swath, expertly delivered, cut deeply into the blue flesh of the demon's shoulder.

"There!" she yelled triumphantly, expecting that the oni's arm would fall away.

Yet, though the naginata cut clear through, she might as well have been cutting water, for the wound sealed itself just as quickly as it formed.

The hannya bared its teeth and laughed.

Another sweep of the naginata cut through the demon's leg. Again the wound sealed itself before she had finished the stroke.

How much longer can I fend this thing off?

Looking to find some vulnerable point within the oni's body, she buried the blade-point into the breast of the beast, but as she did, it seized the shaft with an iron grip. In one motion, the demon turned its body, naginata and all. Yamabuki, who fought to keep a hold on the weapon, was pitched upward—breaking her grasp—throwing her high through the air. She landed in the mud, her wind nearly knocked out. She gasped, half sinking into the cold ooze.

It was then that Yamabuki finally allowed herself to believe that the creature could not be defeated.

Frozen for a moment, not knowing what to do next, Yamabuki watched transfixed as the hannya extracted the naginata from its own chest.

If I am going to die, I refuse to die like a dog on all fours here in the mud. If I die, I die with my sword.

"Come on! Watch me die! I am not afraid," Yamabuki cried as she ran back across the courtyard toward the dimly lit inn and the chamber which held her sword. In one motion the warrior leapt through the open door, dashing back to the bed chamber where she grabbed the still-sheathed long sword. She heard the sound of the hannya as it raged its way through the inn.

All warriors knew that the day of the final battle might come, but to die in an inn under these circumstances? She had never pictured such a fate. She composed herself for what now approached.

The hannya's weighty steps grew louder.

Yamabuki's breathing grew heavy; her mouth became dry, her cheeks flushed. Fear tried to find a wedge, but she resisted it. Her heart pounded harder than she had ever remembered; the blood sang in her ears.

The grim creature appeared at the door, the arrow shafts still protruding from its body. Its laughter verged on hysteria. It moved closer, eyes fixed on Yamabuki. Once again, it tossed the tantō at her feet.

"Die, Kojiro!"

"Die, yourself!" she spat, and in one flash Tiger Claw, her long sword, came out of its scabbard, passed through the beast, cutting a path from its left shoulder to its heart.

It would have been a killing strike for any mortal, so instinctively she pulled the blade from the oni's body, and paused.

The beast moaned, "You are not Kojiro."

At once the oni's ugly features began to recede, and as they faded, the creature let out a piteous sob. "Oh, help me, warrior, save me from this awful eternity. I am lost!"

Yamabuki fought against her own surprise as the demon once again returned to the form of the highborn woman.

Yamabuki managed to gasp, "Help you?"

But already the sad woman began to fade. "I was betrayed. We eloped. We agreed to kill ourselves. I died, but he ran. They buried me in an unmarked grave. No incense was burned; no prayers were said."

She fell to her knees, raised her hands, reaching out—imploring—but she rapidly dissolved into smoke and faded into nothingness.

Yamabuki stood, dripping wet, alone in the empty chamber with her sword still drawn. She was utterly exhausted. The sound of steps reached her consciousness. Over her shoulder she saw the innkeeper at the open door, his mouth agape.

"Go away," she barked. "Can't an inn guest have some privacy!?"

The innkeeper began to stammer.

She glared. "Get out! Or do you want to taste steel?"

He turned on his heel and scampered away.

The warrior sheathed her weapon, but not before examining its edge. It bore not so much as the slightest nick, and what was even more strange, it betrayed no sign of blood. She, herself, was covered head to foot with mud. Mud was in her hair, her ears, under her finger nails.

"So much for my clean kimono," she muttered to herself.

As quickly as she could, she removed the wet kimono, wrapping herself in a dry blanket.

"Samurai-sama?" She heard Kinu's soft voice. "I have brought you a dry kimono." Even in the dim light, she could see Kinu was trembling.

She tried to reassure her. "It is all over, for now. I think you can rest."

Kinu bowed and left the chamber.

After donning the dry kimono, Yamabuki picked up Tiger Claw and set off toward the front of the inn, this time in a more seemly way, and not via the inner court garden.

She peered outside.

No one was in evidence.

Taking her cloak from the entry way, the muddy warrior walked across the courtyard to the open stable gate. Inside she found Hidashi with the colt.

"Kinu said you killed it before it could kill you," he said.

"No, it was not looking for me," she answered.

"She told me you were not hurt."

"All except my shoulder." She reached to touch where the oni's claws had struck—but felt only smooth skin.

This is like some dream.

"You did not run away when I told you to," she said.

"I tried, but I could not leave."

"Hidashi, that was a brave thing you did; brave and smart. Releasing Mochizuki was an excellent decision. And you, old boy . . ." She petted Mochizuki and smiled.

She shook her head. "But next time," she looked into the boy's eyes, "someone distracts a foe and says run away, you *run away.* Do you hear?"

"If I can," he answered meekly.

"Stay here and take care of Mochizuki. I am going to talk to Grandfather."

Having regained her composure somewhat, she headed back to the inn, where she found the innkeeper speaking in whispered tones to Haruyo who was heating more food. A cup of cold saké stood ready on a tray. "I am preparing something warm for you. And there's saké, too." Haruyo smiled.

Yamabuki did not return the smile. Instead she demanded, "Who is Kojiro!"

The innkeeper wrung his hands, "Oh, I knew it. I knew it!"

"And tell me about the woman he was with."

"They left," the old man blurted before Haruyo could say a word. "They left almost right away?" He said it like he did not expect her to believe him.

"What happened to her?"

He stammered, unable to think fast enough.

Yamabuki took a step forward. "I have had more than enough for this evening. Tell me the truth! It is said a samurai will cut out the tongue of a liar." She glared at the innkeeper, trying to make her bluff look real.

The innkeeper slumped down in total defeat.

Haruyo spoke quietly. "She was with a samurai, a handsome man, almost pretty—one called Kojiro. We thought it odd that so high-born a lady should be traveling alone with the likes of him." She paused a moment, embarrassed, then apologized. "*Gomen na-sai.* I meant no insult, only that he was but a lone warrior and we thought she would travel with a retinue. But they had coins and could easily pay, and we thought, 'Who are we to ask? Who are we to question people of high rank?' Yet we knew that something was not right.

"On the night of their stay, the young samurai snuck out to the stables, mounted his steed and left long before dawn and in a great hurry."

The innkeeper began whimpering softly. "It is the end. It will all be found out. It will all be brought out."

Haruyo ignored him. "We, of course, were concerned by this. So we went to her chamber." Haruyo took in a very deep breath as if it would take all she had to say what was next. "We found her dead." And then she exhaled it all, paused, looked down, and continued. "She had taken her own life, or so we thought, for she held her own dagger."

"And what then?" Yamabuki demanded.

"We feared scandal. We feared that we would be punished for having this happen in our inn."

Yamabuki looked at her with suppressed disdain. "And so you buried the body without any rites and in an unmarked grave so that none would know."

Haruyo, for the first time, bowed her head and said, barely above a whisper, "Hai."

"And Hidashi and Kinu? Did they help you in this?"

Haruyo shook her head. "They knew not of it. We wanted to spare them any pain."

"That explains only part of it," Yamabuki challenged.

"Surely, my lady, you have heard the story of women who have loved, but who have died unrequited, returning as devils. It is even said some devils will appear as beautiful women before marriage only to prove themselves to be oni during the wedding night."

Yamabuki glared at Haruyo. "Obviously a story devised by some men."

"Still, you saw the devil-woman. I saw her. So terrifying," Haruyo concluded in a whisper.

"Why then do samurai see an oni?"

"I am not wise in these things, but it is said that the soul of a samurai resides in his swords. I think she seeks the glamour of those who carry swords. It was a samurai who brought her here, and perhaps when she sees the swords she thinks her beloved has returned to her. She was driven to despair. It was her anger and betrayal that you saw. That is why weapons merely passed through her without effect. It couldn't be killed for it was the embodiment of the love that had died; a love that had passed from tenderness to despair. She sought Kojiro to demand justice and for him to fulfill his bargain, his word as a samurai."

"The Gods saved you and us," the innkeeper volunteered.

"It's Gods Absent month—they have left for Izumo Shrine," Yamabuki intoned dryly. "It was Hidashi and Mochizuki who saved me."

"We might have done wrong, but we have been thoroughly punished." The innkeeper nodded resolutely.

"I am tired," Yamabuki said, and looked straight into the old man's eyes. "In the morning, I want you to show me the grave."

"It's among the small copse of trees, behind the stables," Haruyo said with weary sadness.

"And then what will you do, samurai?" the innkeeper asked, his tone uneasy.

"I will do the proper thing."

"And what is that?" His gaze met hers.

"You know. You know perfectly well. I will do what should have been done in the first place." She picked up a pair of chop sticks and threw them down, saying, "I'm tired!"

"Pray for us, too, samurai," Haruyo said as Yamabuki walked into the rainy night. "Pray for each and all of us."

Yamabuki made her way back to the stable. Hidashi was nowhere to be found. She lay down in some hay near Mochizuki, muttering, "I think I would rather be here with you than with them." And with that, she fell into the sleep that had been so rudely interrupted before, and this time she slept without dreaming anything more.

FOUR

RED MAPLES

WHEN YAMABUKI AWOKE, the morning light shone in her eyes.

"Sleeping outside, samurai?"

A woman's voice.

Yamabuki put her hand up to shield herself from the sun's rays. Against the brightening sky, a mounted rider—a warrior—peered down at her in curiosity.

Yamabuki lay on the ground amid tall reeds.

Gathering what dignity she could, she stood up, looking around in bewilderment. She was surrounded by charred timbers.

Mochizuki stood quite near her. Her sword was on the ground, carefully laid out where she had slept. She still wore her full armor as if she had never taken it off the night before, but clearly she could remember doing so.

She remembered everything.

Yamabuki stared at the ruins. "I thought there was an inn here."

"In fact there was," said the mounted warrior, "but it was torched years ago." Yamabuki looked at the silhouetted rider. "A high born lady of the Taira Clan escaped from her parents when she rejected her marriage match. She left with a lover—a handsome young samurai. He took her to the inn that was here. The authorities came after her, but the innkeeper lied, saying he knew nothing of her. But his lies were soon discovered."

"And?" she asked expectantly.

"And?" the mounted warrior repeated flatly. "What do you think? The young lady could not be found, so the authorities decided that the innkeeper and his family were guilty for her disappearance. They were locked inside the inn and the authorities burned the place to the ground."

"Did anyone survive?"

"It is said that everyone perished."

"Even the children?"

"It is said that everyone perished," the other woman repeated.

Yamabuki felt a sharp pang within herself as she remembered the innocent faces of Hidashi and Kinu. "What of the man who was with the Taira lady?"

"They are still looking for him, and the lady, of course. If he's found, he'll be publicly beheaded."

"And the young lady, what happened to her?"

"No one knows. Some say she committed suicide. Some others say the innkeeper's family murdered her for her money. Most think her paramour probably killed her when he tired of her."

"What was her name?"

"Oiwa."

"Do you recall the samurai's name."

"I have forgotten."

"Was he called Kojiro?"

"Perhaps. Kojiro or maybe Jiro. That sounds right, though as I say, I have forgotten." The rider tipped her head quizzically. "How is it that you chose to sleep in these ruins all night? Hardly a peaceful place."

Yamabuki smiled slightly. "I wanted strong saké, good rice, and a warm place to sleep."

"It looks like you did not get any of that," the other woman said with a good-natured laugh.

Yamabuki could now see that the rider was no older than she. Yamabuki grinned. "No, not very much of that."

"Did you see any ghosts?"

Yamabuki did not answer.

"It is said that those who lived here still haunt the place. It is even said two ghost samurai lovers ride through the woods at dusk to warn others not to stay at East Wind Inn."

"Ghostly samurai?"

"They appear along the road where a Buddhist temple once stood. They try to lure others to stay with them for the night. If you do as they suggest, it is said that no one will ever see you again."

Yamabuki brushed straw off her armor.

"May I know your name?" asked the rider.

"Taka Yamabuki."

"Yellow Rose of the Hawk Clan. Excellent name for a warrior! I am called Tomoe, wife of Lord Wada."

They bowed to each other in respect. Then Tomoe turned her horse away. "Perhaps we will meet again one day."

"Perhaps so." Yamabuki watched as the rider and her horse disappeared up the road.

Alone now, she walked across the area she still vividly

remembered as the courtyard, toward the ruins of what had once been the stable. Behind the charred crumbling timbers of the ruin she came upon a cluster of trees. In one she recognized a small piece of weathered cloth not unlike the cloth of the kimono that the beautiful woman had worn the previous night.

She followed a trail that was no more than an open space between the trees. Looking down, she saw the glint of a familiar object protruding from the soil, and for the first time, she picked up the dagger that Oiwa had carried, the dagger that Yamabuki was to have used, as Kojiro's proxy, as the instrument of her own death.

She knew that this was indeed the resting place of the woman who had caused her so much trouble, yet who wanted only love.

As Amaterasu rose in the east, a gentle warm wind caressed the warrior's face. The warrior assembled five wooden markers. With the high born lady's dagger, she carved the name Oiwa on the first marker, placing it on the grave in the quiet clearing. Lighting some of the incense she always carried, Yamabuki proceeded to chant a number of sutras she thought were appropriate for the dead.

Amaterasu was above the trees when these rites were completed. With the same dagger, she inscribed each of the remaining markers with a name: Haruyo, the woman of great dignity who tried to protect her children; Kinu, the brave girl who was so graceful, yet so young; Mikiyasu, the old innkeeper who struggled to make a living, though all the odds had turned against him; and Hidashi, the boy who did not fear the fearless. She placed the markers within the ruins of the inn, chanting sutras she thought would give their souls peace.

Hidashi had said that he could not leave, nor would his sister. Only as she chanted for the freedom of their souls did she begin to understand why they had not left the inn, nor their places within it, for no one had prayed for their souls, either; and she understood, at last, Haruyo's final plea, *Pray for each and all of us.*

Like a samurai, Oiwa's soul, too, was vested in her weapon—a tantō—and like a samurai's sword, Yamabuki placed it, point down, into the earth next to the grave marker.

It was very quiet now. Yamabuki felt peace in the stillness. The air was sweet and warm. Near the end of the Hour of the Dragon, having done all she could do, she collected her belongings and headed up the road lined with maple trees that burned red in the autumn morning. She rode on until the ruins of the inn were completely out of sight, and only then, did she think about where at last she might get strong saké, good rice, and a warm place to sleep for the night.

ILLUSTRATIONS

The illustrations inside this book were drawn from the following historical Japanese works.

"Tale of Genji fifty-four pledge Utsusemi" by Utagawa Hiroshige-ga (1853)

"Battle of Kawanakajima" by Utagawa Kuniyoshi (1854)

"Woman Visiting the Shrine in the Night" by Suzuki Harunobu (18th century)

"Scene from the play Tenjiku Tokubei Karakoto Banashi" by Utagawa Kunisada (also known as Utagawa Toyokuni III) (1849–1853)

"Tomoe, the Female Warrior (Kuchi-e)" by Ogata Gekko (1900)

A Note from the Author

Cold Saké was written during the especially dark and spooky New England autumn of 1986. I wrote it in response to a contest. The call was for a short story of under 6,000 words.

The main character, Taka Yamabuki, started to form in my mind, and the more I researched the Heian era (when the actual woman whom history books referred to as Yamabuki lived), the more involved I became with who she was and the world in which she lived.

The short story grew to novelette length and so unsurprisingly I never did submit the original draft for consideration.

Soon the Yamabuki character grew into a projected five volume series and 180,000 words covering the first book and a half, eclipsing the novelette.

Though Taka Yamabuki of *Cold Saké* is completely consistent and recognizable, it is set outside of the events of the other novels, current and planned. Wanting to share the ghost story, Toot Sweet Ink is publishing *Cold Saké* as a standalone book.

I can just picture Yamabuki in her old age gathering a group of youngsters together, and with a sly smile on her face saying, "Let me tell you a story that happened to me when I was young. And I swear it's all true. . . ."

KML
Boulder, 2015

GLOSSARY

Akitsushima: The Autumn Creek Land; Japan.

Akitsushima no Monogatari: Tales of the Autumn Creek Land.

Amaterasu: Sun goddess; synonymous with the sun.

ebira: Arrow quiver.

Emma: Reagent of the underworld.

engawa: An outer walkway of a building.

Gods Absent Month: 10th Lunar Month; in current times, November.

gomen nasai: I am sorry; forgive me.

haguro: Blackening teeth to indicate marriage.

hai: Yes.

hakama: Split trouser-skirt.

hannya: Monster; Devil-woman.

Hō: Old Japanese name for China.

Izumo Shrine: Sacred shrine near the medieval capital.

jigai: Suicide; self-disposal *(literal)*.

jigoku: Buddhist hell.

jimbaori: Field marshal's coat.

Jizō: Patron and guardian of dead children's souls.

Lady Sei Shonagon: Japanese diarist, 966–1017.

Makura no Samurai: Pillow Book of a Samurai.

naginata: Medium-length sword blade affixed to a long pole; sometimes compared to a halberd or a glaive.

obi: Sash worn around the waist.

Oku: The wilderness. The back country.

oni: Devil; troll.

onna: Woman.

oshiroi: White rice-powder make-up.

pillow book: Diary.

ryokai: Arrow with head shaped like a crescent.

saya: Scabbard.

shaku: Length of about a foot.

shitagi: Inner kimono, similar to an undergarment.

tachi: Long sword often used by cavalry.

tantō: Dirk; dagger.

Ushi-Tora: Mythical beast, half-bull, half-tiger, that lives at Demon's Gate.

Wa: Old Chinese name for Japan.

wakizashi: Medium-length sword.

Yellow Land: The underworld.

JAPANESE YEARS, SEASONS, AND TIME

SOLAR STEMS

	Romanji	*Kanji*	*Start Date*	*Name*
1	Risshun	立春	February 4	Beginning of spring
2	Usui	雨水	February 18	Rain water
3	Keichitsu	啓蟄	March 5	Awakening of Insects
4	Shunbun	春分	March 20	Vernal equinox
5	Seimei	清明	April 4	Clear and bright
6	Kokuu	穀雨	April 20	Grain rain
7	Rikka	立夏	May 5	Beginning of summer
8	Shōman	小満	May 21	Grain Fills
9	Bōshu	芒種	June 5	Grain in Ear
10	Geshi	夏至	June 21	Summer Solstice
11	Shōsho	小暑	July 7	Little Heat
12	Taisho	大暑	July 23	Great Heat
13	Risshū	立秋	August 7	Beginning of Autumn
14	Shosho	処暑	August 23	End of Heat
15	Hakuro	白露	September 7	Descent of White Dew
16	Shūbun	秋分	September 23	Autumnal Equinox
17	Kanro	寒露	October 8	Cold Dew
18	Sōkō	霜降	October 23	Descent of Frost
19	Rittō	立冬	November 7	Beginning of winter
20	Shōsetsu	小雪	November 22	Little Snow
21	Taisetsu	大雪	December 7	Great Snow
22	Tōji	冬至	December 22	Winter Solstice
23	Shōkan	小寒	January 5	Little Cold
24	Daikan	大寒	January 20	Great Cold

Japanese Years

Kiūan 1–6   Jan 25, 1145 to Jan 19, 1151
Kiūan 5 has a 13th month observed starting July 18, 1148

Nimbiō 1–3   Jan 20, 1151 to Feb 13, 1154
Nimbiō 1 has a 13th month observed starting May 18, 1151
Nimbiō 3 has a 13th month observed starting Jan 16, 1154

Kiūju 1–2   Feb 14, 1154 to Jan 20, 1156

Hōgen 1–3   Jan 21, 1156 to Jan 20, 1159
Hōgen 1 has a 13th month observed starting Oct 16, 1156

Heiji 1   Jan 21, 1159 to Feb 8, 1160
Heiji 1 has a 13th month observed starting June 18, 1159

Eiriaku 1   Feb 9, 1160 to Jan 27, 1161

Ōhō 1–2   Jan 28, 1161 to Feb 4, 1163
Ōhō 2 has a 13th month observed starting April 17, 1162

Chōkwan 1–2   Feb 5, 1163 to Feb 12, 1165
Chōkwan 2 has a 13th month observed starting Dec 16, 1164

Eiman 1   Feb 13, 1165 – Feb 2, 1166

Nin-an 1–3   Feb 3, 1166 to Jan 29, 1169
Nin-an 2 has a 13th month observed starting August 17, 1167

Kaō 1–2   Jan 30, 1169 to Feb 6, 1171

Shōan 1–4   Feb 7, 1171 to Jan 23, 1175
Shōan 2 has a 13th month observed starting January 16, 1173

Angen 1–2   Jan 24, 1175 to Jan 31, 1177
Angen 1 has a 13th month observed starting October 17, 1175

JAPANESE HOURS

Hour	Bell Strikes	Solar time
Rabbit	6	5 – 7 AM
Dragon	5	7 – 9 AM
Snake	4	9 – 11 AM
Horse	9	11 AM – 1 PM *(Noon)*
Sheep	8	1 – 3 PM
Monkey	7	3 – 5 PM
Bird	6	5 – 7 PM
Dog – *Shokō, First Watch*	5	7 – 9 PM
Pig – *Nikō, Second Watch*	4	9 – 11 PM
Mouse – *Saukō, Third Watch*	9	11 PM – 1 AM *(Midnight)*
Ox – *Shikō, Fourth Watch*	8	1 – 3 AM *("witching hour")*
Tiger – *Gokō, Fifth Watch*	7	3 – 5 AM

NOTE: The hours of the day are defined as divisions of time between sunrise and sunset, and back to sunrise again. There are six Japanese hours in each day and six each night. The sun always rises in the Hour of the Rabbit, and sets in the Hour of the Bird. Naturally, as the seasons change, nighttime and daytime hours will vary in actual duration, daytime hours longer during the summer, nighttime hours longer during the winter. Averaged out over the year, each "hour" works out to be approximately two of our modern hours.

ABOUT THE AUTHOR

Katherine M. Lawrence is a student of martial arts and things Japanese. She graduated from the University of Washington with a BA degree in both History and Chemistry, then continued working on her Masters in History at the Far Eastern and Slavic Institute, and received an MBA from Harvard University.

She is currently developing further books about the adventures of Yamabuki.

Kate on Twitter: @pingkate

Kate's blog: KateLore.com

Kate's newsletter signup: eepurl.com/K8IIf

EXTRA

EXCERPT FROM: COLD BLOOD

Book One of the exciting Yamabuki adventure, *Sword of the Taka Samurai*

Sixteen years old, Yamabuki embarks upon her first mission: to deliver important dispatches to the capital. Untested and traveling alone, Yamabuki enters a world of natural beauty, unusual characters, unexpected friendships, and indiscriminate brutality and violence. But unbeknown to her, a ninja assassin is on her trail. And before she knows it, her life hangs in the balance.

EXCERPT FROM **COLD BLOOD:**
ARE MY TEETH BLACK?

4 bell strikes
First quarter, Hour of the Snake
Full Moon of New Life Month

The Kanmon Strait

IN PRISTINE BATTLE ARMOR, traveling without her personal guards or handmaids, not wearing any insignia that revealed her exact rank, Yamabuki at last stood in her own right on the promontory that looked north across the Barrier Strait.

The rising sun burned so bright that the heavens scarcely looked blue. Shimmering light shone all the way across the vast Windward Sea which flowed off the edge of the world at the eastern horizon.

A moist westerly breeze caressed the warrior's young face, leaving the slightest taste of brine on her lips and the fresh scent of fish and kelp in her nostrils.

Mochizuki, her jet-black two-year-old colt, snorted his displeasure.

"I know you don't like the wind," she whispered, reaching up to stroke his mane with one hand while tightening her grip on his bridle with the other. His hot wet breath blew across her hand.

As with all horses, his hearing was keen and he grew fretful when anything impeded it.

She wondered to what extent his disquiet had infected her. Ever since crossing into Chikuzen Province two days before, her mount had grown increasingly temperamental—possibly because the North Road from Mizuki to Kita had teemed with people, horses, carts, wagons, and livestock. Disguised as a common samurai, more or less blending into the throng, Yamabuki trusted that she had escaped notice. However, if someone was shadowing her, it would have been easy enough for them to meld in as well.

This morning she dismissed her earlier apprehensions as mere fancy and instead looked ahead. She strained to make out the opposite shore through the thin, lingering haze, which washed out the details of the Main Isle of Honshu, her destination.

A voice startled her. "'Better to cross the strait as the sun rises than as she sets.' At least that's how the commoners put it." The voice belonged to a man who not only had the temerity to interject himself into a nonexistent conversation with her, but even had the impertinence to approach her along her horse's opposite flank, the samurai's blindside.

Since Mochizuki stood between her and the stranger, at first all she could see was the man's muddy sandals and loose-fitting cotton trousers, blue-on-white, with the *ine* rice plant pattern.

She immediately stepped around her mount, her left hand near, but not exactly on, her sword hilt. Her eyes met the stranger's.

He's not even armed, let alone warrior class.

He had a ruddy face. Handsome in a rugged way. A bit older than she. Kindly bloodshot eyes which were happy and sad all at the same time.

Odd. A rich man's sandals, but a commoner's tunic.

As he grinned, his eyes smiled. He may have noticed her sword hand. "I was just behind you on the road all the way up from Kita. Wasn't following," he assured. "Just going to the trailhead."

He cast his gaze toward Honshu. "Boatmen call this place Dragon's Throat. It's the shortest distance between the Great Isles. The two seas somehow know it, too, and so they rush through the channel. In the end, the shortest distance to land has the strongest currents."

She moved her hand away from her weapon.

He tossed a wrist in a casual gesture toward the north eastern horizon. "Beautiful morning for it though. We are both crossing the barrier, no?"

Resolute, she looked across the turbid expanse. Seemingly lost in the idea of crossing, finally she answered softly, almost to herself, "I haven't traveled for ten days and nights for just a view."

"Ha-ha!" he laughed, respectfully looking her up and down. "White crossed arrow-feather insignia on indigo. You are of the Taka clan from Great Bay Province . . . from the southeastern tip, yes?"

"As far from here as it is possible to be, yet still be on the same isle."

"*Hai*, but not for long." His eyes narrowed. "Hear that?" He tilted his head, his ear toward the sea.

She found that for the moment she could hear nothing more than the hum of a steady wind mingling with the soft pulse of the sea and the occasional screeches of wheeling gulls. Since her battle helmet concealed her hair gathered up under its steel crown, if she removed her *kabuto* to improve her hearing, her long locks would be released and everyone would immediately see that she was a female, and a young one at that. But then, a moment later, shouts drifted up from the water below.

The man beckoned her to the sea cliff's edge. "My ears aren't actually *that* good," he said, pointing over the side. "I saw the cargo boat enter the cove."

She peered down the nearly vertical drop-off of gray clay and rock.

Far below, a festively decorated shallow-draught *kobune*, crammed to capacity with about forty warriors, tacked toward shore. Its *senchou* skillfully guided his craft through the swirling whitish-blue current that streamed out to sea. As he maneuvered the kobune toward the wooden landing, thick rope coils flew from the boat to waiting hands on the shore. In the splendidly open air, the voices of the shore crew's calling-song carried up from below, echoing off the surrounding crescent cliffs.

> *Haul, haul. Heave-ho! Heave-ho!*
> *Put your backs in. Dokkoisho!*
> *Though the gulls call us*
> *We cannot tarry*
> *Pretty girls we wait to marry*
> *(Please wait, please wait.)*

Steadily the haulers drew the craft out of the tidal basin and toward the calmer waters near the decaying timbers of the makeshift dock. Though weathered by salt spray and the pounding sun, and feasted upon by all manner of marine bores, the pier's rough-hewn pilings were still sturdy enough for lashing and securing the boat. The lines were hardly tied when the contingent of samurai leapt onto the dock.

"Looks like an invasion," Yamabuki said drolly.

The man in the white-on-blue kimono laughed, for they both knew it was nothing of the kind. The warriors were merely glad that they had reached their destination and could at last escape the wave-tossed kobune. Doubled over on the rocky beach, three of the passengers joined into the ancient and unwelcome ritual of losing the contents of their stomachs.

"They didn't drink enough saké," he breathed.

"For courage?" She looked askance.

"No," he said seriously, "you drink it because it makes the land move like the sea. If you've drunk enough before you board, once you're out on the water, you can't tell the difference. You won't get seasick."

He reached into his copious sleeve, where he dug around until his face brightened. "This one's full." He pulled out an ornate porcelain flask with the ine emblem painted on its side. Raising the saké bottle high, he breathed, "It's what you'll need to cross the barrier."

He hummed, rolling his tongue across his lips.

"Good saké. Strong." He smiled more broadly as he unstoppered the flask and offered the bottle's now naked neck to her.

With a subtle gesture of her small finger, she indicated for him to take it away.

He shook the bottle hard enough that she could hear the saké slosh inside. "If we don't drink together, it will mean you have no friends."

To most people, at least of her class, a person's mouth was considered to be unclean. A vile thing. Contact with another's mouth, or whatever it touched, was unthinkable to all but the most wanton. Even the practice of mouth-sucking was usually confined to the bedchamber, and then only between married people or among lovers.

Yamabuki shook her head.

"I do not have any sickness, if that's what you think," he huffed.

"I'm not thirsty," she replied, her eyes slightly drawn, but expressing a modest smile of politeness.

Far below, the seasick warriors eventually recovered and chased after their fellows, who already were headed up the steep cliff-trail.

"They're Ōuchi clan." He gulped down a generous mouthful of saké and continued, "And low-ranking ones at that."

"And how do you know this?"

"For one, the *hanabishi* insignia on their banner flags. The diamond-flower is the Ōuchi clan symbol."

"That doesn't declare their rank."

"No." He nodded, looking pleased with his own perspicacity, which he celebrated with another swig. "It does not, but that boat carries a horse-blind, yet they don't have a horse amongst them. They even packed some of their number into the kobune's stable." He twisted his nose into a sign of a disgusting smell. "As I said, low ranking. Samurai of importance ride horses. The better the horse, the higher their status," he said, shooting a glance at Mochizuki.

Although he had readily recognized her clan crest, had offered her saké, and had even spoken to her about the "common people," as if they were the "other," the two of them had not exchanged names, nor were they likely to. Such niceties were practiced, of course, only by those of the *buké* warrior class and the *kuge* aristocratic class—in short, among those who had clan affiliations to begin with and therefore had something to announce. Their honored names were derived from being of high rank while in service of a local ruler, or were handed down to the progeny of the various branches of the imperial households.

Even then, disclosing one's names and titles was not done without a specific reason. Such reasons could vary, from forming a lifelong friendship all the way to initiating a duel to the death. In the latter case the combatants would, before ever drawing steel, announce not only their clan and personal names, but their titles and, above all, their impressive string of victories, real or embellished.

But when it came to commoners, what good would it be to exchange names? The upper classes called them *nanigashi*, the thus-and-such people—names such as carpenter, woodcutter, fisherman, *kago* runner, combined with some mundane personal name: Tree, Mountain, River, First Born, Second Born, Young Cattle, and so forth.

Hardly worth taking the time to remember.

The man with the saké bottle did not fit into any immediately identifiable commoner category. Still, she was unwilling to exchange names with him, though she wanted to refer to him in some way, if only to herself.

Yamabuki eyed him. Because of his blue kimono with its rice plant pattern, she gave him a sobriquet: *Aoi Ine*. Blue Rice.

He lifted his flask and took a drink. "Sure you don't want any?"

Again Yamabuki politely declined.

With that, Blue Rice turned and moved away from the bluff. "Well then, it shall not be long now. My sister awaits me across the channel. If I don't miss my guess, the senchou will be shoving off soon enough. They never wait for very long." He smiled wistfully.

"I shall see you down to the dock," he said over his shoulder as he walked away.

Yamabuki looked askance. "Not taking the trail?"

"The road."

"That's longer," she called after him.

"Reminiscence," he shouted back and disappeared around the downhill bend.

She looked at the empty road, shaking her head. *I suppose this is how common people speak. Even if Blue Rice thought I was merely of the buké class, his manners are so forward!*

Has he been following me? Not just now—since Mizuki. Maybe even before. Is he aware of the mission I am on?

Whether he was a spy or was not, whether he knew the purpose of her journey or not, there was no turning back.

Yamabuki retightened the binding cords of the straw protecting Mochizuki's hooves, cinched her own helmet cords, took her mount's reins, and headed toward the awaiting kobune.

Cold Blood is available now!

About Toot Sweet Ink

Toot Sweet Ink is an imprint of Toot Sweet Inc., an independent publisher based in Boulder, Colorado.

Watch for our upcoming releases in historical fiction, science fiction, women's contemporary fiction, humor, and non-fiction—and more Yamabuki stories by Katherine M. Lawrence.

TootSweetInk.com

@TootSweetInk

facebook.com/tootsweetink

Sign up for our Inkvine newsletter to get updates and learn about new releases and discount opportunities on our upcoming titles!

eepurl.com/K8XVn